THE CAPTAIN

DISCARD

THE CAPTAIN

CHRIS KREIE

darbycreek

MINNEAPOLIS

Darby Creek
A division of Lerner Publishing Group, Inc.
241 First Avenue North
Minneapolis, MN 55401 USA

For reading levels and more information, look up this title at www.lernerbooks.com.

The images in this book are used with the permission of: iStock.com/thomas-bethge; iStock.com/Purdue9394; iStock.com/PhonlamaiPhoto; iStock.com/sumnersgraphicsinc.

Main body text set in Janson Text LT Std 12/17.5.
Typeface provided by Adobe Systems.

Library of Congress Cataloging-in-Publication Data

Names: Kreie, Chris, author.
Title: The captain / written by Chris Kreie.
Description: Minneapolis : Darby Creek, [2018] | Series: Kick! | Summary: "When a scandal upsets the high school soccer team, the captain, Malik, struggles to bring his team back together and learn to trust a new coach"— Provided by publisher.
Identifiers: LCCN 2017021456 (print) | LCCN 2017037508 (ebook) | ISBN 9781541500280 (eb pdf) | ISBN 9781541500228 (lb : alk. paper) | ISBN 9781541500273 (pb : alk. paper)
Subjects: | CYAC: Soccer—Fiction. | Leadership—Fiction. | Teamwork (Sports)—Fiction. | Conduct of life—Fiction. | High schools—Fiction. | Schools—Fiction.
Classification: LCC PZ7.K8793 (ebook) | LCC PZ7.K8793 Cap 2018 (print) | DDC [Fic]—dc23

LC record available at https://lccn.loc.gov/2017021456

Manufactured in the United States of America
1-43654-33471-8/30/2017

For Sammie, my daughter and friend, whose kindness and virtue shine brightly.

MALIK charged down the middle of the field toward the net. He watched his friend and teammate Logan dribble the ball up the right side of the field. "Keep possession!" he yelled. "Stay under control!" Malik sprinted past his defender and stopped at the edge of the box. His defender was playing him tight. If he kept running, he would be offside when Logan passed him the ball. "Pass back to the circle!" he yelled. "Then reverse it!"

Malik's team, the Gators, was taking on the Sharks from Gulf Coast High. It was the Gators' fourth game of the season and they were riding a three-game winning streak.

Malik waited near the penalty arc. Logan passed to a teammate in the corner and then received the ball back. Malik inched forward, slowly and quietly, hoping to avoid his defender's attention.

Logan dribbled away from the goal. His defender was playing him loose, giving Logan the opportunity to survey the action and see who was open. He kicked it toward the middle of the field. A midfielder for the Gators then kicked the ball wide to the left.

Malik was beginning to get impatient. He had already scored one goal and was hungry for another. But he remembered the advice Coach Washington had given him: "Don't hurry," he had said. "Don't rush. Sometimes you have to slow down and let the play come to you."

It was important to play smart. Malik knew that. Good goal scorers put the ball in the back of the net because they think ahead two or three passes. All the soccer greats were intelligent players, and Malik prided himself on his soccer brain. And as the team captain, his patience had paid off for him before.

Malik's teammate on the left suddenly lofted a long pass across the field back to

Logan near the right sideline. He trapped the ball and then controlled it. He looked at Malik and that was all it took—their minds were in sync. Since the two of them had played together since kindergarten, they often communicated on the field without even talking. Logan quickly danced around his defender as Malik shuffled to his right. "Forward!" shouted Malik.

Logan passed the ball toward the net at the exact moment Malik blasted past his defender. Malik met the ball and then dribbled forward toward the right corner of the net. The goalie stayed back. *Big mistake*, thought Malik as he measured the angle. *You should've come out to challenge me.* He moved forward and then unleashed the kick. The ball stayed low as it headed toward the far corner of the net. The goalie didn't stand a chance. He dove for the ball but was much too late. The ball slammed into the netting.

"Yes!" cried Malik.

Logan rushed toward Malik and they celebrated with their teammates in a mob.

The Gators had opened up a 2–0 lead on the Sharks.

Soccer was everything to Malik. He'd been playing since he could walk and was rarely seen without a ball. Coaches had noticed him from an early age. His skills were always far better than other players his age: When he was seven, he played with the ten-year-olds. As an eighth grader, he was moved up to the varsity team. In his junior year, he set the record for most goals ever scored at Greenville High.

This was his senior year—his final and most important season with the Gators. Letters from college coaches had been arriving at his house since tenth grade. It was pretty clear that Malik was going to play college soccer, but the only school that really mattered to him was East Coast University. They were defending national champions and the biggest soccer powerhouse in the country. Malik had his path all figured out: get a scholarship to East Coast U, win the national championship, then make it to the pros. But if he wanted this to happen, he had to continue scoring goals, being a leader, and doing everything within his power to carry his team to the state title.

Late in the game Malik returned the favor to Logan by setting him up for a goal. The two of them had scored all three of the Gators' goals. The game against the Sharks ended with the Gators winning 3–0.

"I don't think we're going to lose a game all season," said Logan after the teams shook hands. Malik and Logan walked toward the bench.

"Let's not get ahead of ourselves," said Malik. "We need to take things one game at a time."

"Okay, Coach." Logan laughed and gave Malik a playful punch to the chest.

"You're right, though," said Malik. "If we play every game the way we played today, nobody can stop us."

"I like the sound of that," said Logan.

"Hey, Malik!" It was Coach Washington. "Over here."

"See you in a second," said Malik as he turned and jogged toward his coach.

"Another great game," said his coach. "Add two more goals to your total."

"It's the win that counts," said Malik.

"That's what I like to hear." Coach Washington put his arm around Malik's shoulder. "What did you learn out there? What did you guys do wrong?"

This was their routine. The two of them took time to talk after every game. Coach would point out a few things the team did well, but more importantly, he wanted Malik to identify things the team could do to get better. Malik loved playing for Coach Washington. The two of them had bonded immediately when Malik was called up to play on varsity. Coach loved Malik's determination and work ethic, and Malik loved how Coach pushed him to be the best possible player he could be. They spent so much time together and had become so close over the past five years that Coach Washington was like a second father to Malik.

"We left ourselves open for counterattacks," said Malik. "There were at least three times I can remember when too many of our guys rushed the net. If the Sharks were a better team, they would have made a counter and caught us out of position."

"I couldn't agree more," said Coach Washington. "Those mistakes could cost us a win in the playoffs. You'll talk to the guys about it at practice tomorrow?"

"For sure."

"Great," said Coach. "We played well, but it was far from a perfect game. There's always room for improvement."

"Agreed," said Malik.

"And remember, don't play fast . . ."

"Play smart," Malik interrupted.

Coach laughed. "Get out of here!"

Malik smiled and ran toward his teammates.

MALIK walked into first period history class the following morning with a skip in his step. He was still riding high from the victory over the Sharks the day before and history was his favorite. Coach Washington was the teacher and many of his teammates were in the class.

"Malik!" Logan called to him from the back row. Coach Washington didn't believe in assigned seats so Malik and Logan always sat together. He walked to the empty seat beside Logan.

Coach Washington walked through the door and placed a stack of books on the front table. "Good morning, everyone." He took off his jacket and hung it on the back of his chair.

"Morning, Coach!" shouted Logan.

"Coach of the year!" added Daniel, another player from the soccer team.

"Start polishing the trophy!" yelled Malik.

The rest of the students laughed.

"Yeah, yeah. All right now." Coach Washington smiled. "Keep it on the soccer field, gentlemen. In here it's all about European history."

"But Coach," said Malik. "Didn't Europeans invent soccer?"

"Yeah," said Logan. "In the old days? You know, back in history?"

More laughter.

"That's actually a really interesting question," said Coach Washington. "Soccer is said to have gotten its start in several countries, including China, Egypt, and Greece."

"Greece!" said Logan. "That's in Europe."

"True," said Coach Washington. He walked behind the podium and flipped on the computer projector. "But today our topic is not the Greeks or the invention of soccer. Instead we will be covering the start of World War I. Everyone open up your textbooks to page eighty-seven."

Malik grabbed his history book from his backpack. He knew absolutely nothing about World War I, but he knew Coach would make it interesting.

***

At the start of practice later that day Coach Washington led the team through warm-ups. After some stretching and sprints, they ran through a cone drill they did nearly every practice. It was Coach's favorite because it improved their footwork and overall quickness.

As Coach pushed them through the drill, many of the players began to tire. "Pick up the pace, Freshman!" barked Coach Washington. He was yelling at Omar, one of only two freshmen to make the varsity team. Throughout the drill, Omar had been coming in last in his group. "You keep running like that I'm going to have to send you back to junior varsity. That's a pathetic display of speed." Coach Washington could be pretty hard on the guys. Some players took Coach's comments personally, but they didn't bother Malik. He liked to be pushed. He credited his own success to Coach's intensity. Malik believed it was because of his training under Coach Washington that he was going to have a real shot at playing soccer for a big-time university next year.

Omar sprinted past the cone and collapsed to the ground. Coach Washington ran over to him. "On your feet, Freshman!" he yelled. "On your feet!" Omar stood up. Coach got into his face. "This isn't a picnic. We don't take naps in the grass. Five laps! Now!" Omar wiped the sweat from his face and began running toward the far end of the field.

Coach Washington looked at the other guys. "Any of the rest of you planning on taking it easy out here?"

"No, Coach!" they yelled.

"Good!" Coach Washington walked to Malik and handed him the whistle. Because Malik was captain, Coach often had him lead some of the drills. "Take over, Malik. Run 'em hard." Coach walked to the far sidelines.

"Next group up!" called Malik. "On my signal!" He blew the whistle and watched as the guys dug their feet into the turf and raced from cone to cone. He took his role as captain seriously and made sure nobody slacked off. "Hard work here will pay off in the games!"

The players in that group finished quickly, and Logan was the first to get back to his cone.

"I'm in!" Malik said, tossing the whistle to Logan and taking his position between two of the cones. Five other guys lined up with him.

"Who's going to beat me?" shouted Malik to the other participants. He smiled.

Tweet! Logan blew the whistle.

Malik tore across the turf, digging his feet into the grass and pushing off hard with his legs. He made it to the first cone. He slammed on the brakes, touched the cone, and spun his body the other direction. He could see his teammates out of the corner of his eye. It was going to be close. He put his head down and thrust his arms forward, flying past the cone before anyone else reached it.

"Not today!" Malik shouted. "But nice hustle everyone!" He bent over to catch his breath. "Okay, guys! Grab some water then meet at the center circle."

Malik joined Logan and the rest of the players on the sidelines to grab a drink. He reached into his bag and took a long drink from his water bottle, draining every drop. The sun was intense, soaking his hair and making his T-shirt damp with sweat.

"Hey," said Logan, nudging Malik. "What's going on over there?"

"What?" asked Malik. Logan was looking across to the opposite sideline.

"Why is Mr. Randall here?" asked Logan. "And Mr. Wiggins?"

Malik turned his head. Sure enough, the athletic director, Mr. Randall, and the principal, Mr. Wiggins, were standing with Coach Washington on the other side of the field. "I have no idea."

Malik and Logan watched as Mr. Randall and Mr. Wiggins talked with Coach Washington.

"Coach doesn't look very happy," said Malik.

By this time, the entire team was watching. Mr. Wiggins and Coach Washington were getting into each other's faces. Mr. Randall stepped in, and then Coach put both hands up in front of him as if to say he was giving in. He then turned and stormed away, making a beeline toward the teacher parking lot.

"What in the world?" asked Malik. He and Logan looked at each other in confusion.

Mr. Wiggins and Mr. Randall walked over to the players. "Boys," said Mr. Randall, "here's what's up. Mr. Wiggins is going to bring a few players to his office and they're going to have a chat. The rest of you will continue with your practice."

"What happened to Coach?" asked Malik.

"Let's do this first," said Mr. Randall.

"We deserve to know," said Logan.

"And you will know," said Mr. Randall. "But right now we need these players to join Mr. Wiggins." He looked at a slip of paper in his hand. "Daniel, Logan, and Hudefa."

All eyes turned to the three players.

"What did we do?" protested Daniel. His eyes were angry.

"Why us?" asked Logan.

"We'll talk about that inside," said Mr. Wiggins.

Malik was frozen. He had absolutely no clue why three of his teammates, including his best friend, were being asked to leave practice with the school principal. *What kind of trouble are they in?* he thought. *And why did Coach leave practice so abruptly?* The whole thing seemed like a bad dream.

"This is a bunch of garbage!" snapped Daniel, with venom in his voice.

"Watch your tone, son," said Mr. Randall.

The accused boys stood still and stared defiantly at Mr. Randall, ignoring his directions to follow Mr. Wiggins inside. Malik knew the three of them were angry and confused, but that was still no reason to disrespect their principal and athletic director. "Do what they ask," Malik said forcefully to his teammates. "Go with Mr. Wiggins."

Daniel shot him a laser-like glare. "Who

do you think you are?" he asked. "My father? You can't tell me what to do."

"I'm not your father," said Malik. "But I am your captain, and right now you need to do what you're being told."

"Get over yourself," said Daniel. "I do what I want to do, when I want to do it."

Logan grabbed Daniel by the shoulder. "Let's go," said Logan. "Let's get this cleared up." He began pulling Daniel toward the school. Hudefa followed Logan's lead and the three of them finally headed inside with Mr. Wiggins.

Daniel turned and shot one final menacing stare in Malik's direction.

Malik watched them walk away. He and Daniel had never been good friends, but they certainly weren't enemies either. Daniel had never acted this way before. It was almost as if he was angry because he knew why Mr. Wiggins wanted to talk to him. It seemed as if Daniel knew he was guilty of something. *But if Daniel is guilty, does that make Logan guilty too?* Malik had absolutely no idea what was going on.

"GENTLEMEN," said Mr. Randall after Logan and the others had disappeared into the school. "Everyone have a seat."

Malik looked around. It seemed weird to be taking directions on the soccer field from someone other than Coach Washington. His teammates must have felt the same way because no one moved. Malik's captain instincts kicked in again. "Everyone!" he shouted. "Sit down!"

The players listened to him and quickly sat down in the grass.

"Thanks, Malik," said Mr. Randall. He waited until the players were ready. "I want to tell you this now, while I have you all together. And I want you to hear it straight from me without the rumors." He paused. "This isn't easy to tell you, but Coach Washington will no longer be your coach. He's going to be leaving Greenville High."

The players looked at each other in shock.

"What are you talking about?" Malik stood up. "What do you mean leaving?"

"I've asked him to resign from his position."

What? thought Malik. *This can't be true.* "You mean you've fired him?" asked Malik.

"I know this comes as a surprise," said Mr. Randall.

What on Earth has Coach done? "And what about our teammates?" he asked, panicked. "What did they do? What's going to happen to them?"

"I can't go into that," said Mr. Randall. "I need to respect the boys' privacy. All I can tell you is we received some very serious information from two extremely trustworthy sources. This will all be out in the open soon, and when it is, you will have all the information you need. Right now you need to keep practicing, keep playing soccer, and try to keep your mind off of all this."

"We can't do that," said Malik. "This is our coach, those are our teammates—we deserve more answers *now*." His voice was cracking with emotion.

Mr. Randall shook his head. "I'm sorry, but I've said everything I can say. Right now I've got to get inside and sit down with Mr. Wiggins and the others." He turned his back and headed toward the school.

Malik and his teammates were frozen. *Coach wouldn't do anything to damage the team*, thought Malik. *This has to be some kind of mistake.* He stood motionless on the field, a mixed-up ball of anger, confusion, and worry.

***

One of the assistant coaches ran the rest of practice, but it was pointless. Everyone just went through the motions. Malik's mind was not on passes and shots and defensive technique. The only thing running through his head was Coach Washington and what possible serious things Mr. Wiggins thought he had done. All he wanted was to finish practice, call Logan, and get some answers.

Malik tried calling him a couple of times on his drive home, but Logan didn't pick up. *Is he avoiding me?* Malik thought. *Is he ashamed about what he did or is there a chance he's angry with me for some reason?* It wasn't until Malik got to his bedroom that Logan finally answered his calls.

"What happened?" Malik asked him.

"We got suspended," said Logan. "For five games. I'm so angry, I don't know what to do with myself."

"Suspended?" asked Malik. The news hit him like a freight train. No one had ever been suspended from the soccer team since he had been at Greenville. "All three of you?"

"Yep."

"What for?" asked Malik.

"Mr. Wiggins says we cheated," said Logan. "He said Coach gave us the answers to some tests."

"And that's why Coach got fired?"

"Apparently."

Malik's head was spinning. He couldn't believe what he was hearing. *Coach would never help players cheat*, he thought. *But Mr. Wiggins wouldn't have fired him without some kind of proof, right?* "It's not true, is it?" he asked.

"Of course not," said Logan defiantly. "We didn't do it."

"Then why are they saying you did?"

"They have something against Coach," said Logan. "Mr. Wiggins never liked him. Once Coach started being successful, Mr. Wiggins was just looking for a way to get rid of him."

That explanation didn't make any sense to Malik. *Mr. Wiggins had something against Coach because he was a winner? Really? That's hard to believe.* "So you think they just made the whole thing up?" he asked.

"Well, Coach did help us on some tests," said Logan. "That's true. But he just helped us learn the stuff. We didn't cheat."

Malik didn't know what to think. He wanted to believe Logan, but what he was saying wasn't logical. *Why would Mr. Wiggins lie? Why would he invent a big, elaborate cheating scandal just to get Coach Washington fired?* Mr. Wiggins was a good guy. A solid guy. The story from Logan didn't add up. *Could it be possible that Coach really had helped the players cheat? And that Logan cheated too?*

"What are you going to do?" Malik asked.

"We're going to fight it," said Logan. "And get Coach his job back."

Malik didn't know what to say.

"You're in, right?" asked Logan.

Malik stuttered. "Of course."

"Good," said Logan. "I'm going to call the other guys. I'll talk to you more tomorrow."

After Logan hung up, Malik sat stunned on his bed. When he had woken up earlier that morning, he never would have thought his day would turn out like this.

THE next day, there was a substitute teacher for history class.

"I'm still so angry Coach was fired," said Logan before class started. "He got a bad deal. There's absolutely no doubt in my mind about that."

Malik had spent the whole night racking his brain. *Maybe Mr. Wiggins was just confused about the whole thing*, he had finally decided. *Someone must have given him bad information.* He remained convinced there was no way Coach would've cheated and risked the future of the team. "I've been thinking," said Malik. He leaned toward Logan. "The whole thing isn't fair. The school can't fire a guy just like that. They can't fire Coach without giving him a chance to tell his side of the story. Can they?"

Daniel laughed. He had been eavesdropping on their conversation. He leaned back in his chair, his arms folded across his body. "This school isn't a democracy, man. We're part of a dictatorship here at Greenville. Don't you know that?"

Malik ignored him. "We could go to the school board," he continued to Logan. "Ask them to at least hear Coach out?"

"I don't know," said Logan.

"We need to find out who lied to Mr. Wiggins about Coach cheating," said Malik. "Get them to confess and tell the truth."

"Take a look at Sherlock Holmes over here." Daniel laughed again. "Thinking he can find the clues and solve the mystery."

"Stay out of this, Daniel," Malik snapped back. He turned back to Logan. "What do you think?"

"It sounds complicated," he said.

"Don't you want to clear your name and get Coach back?" asked Malik.

"Of course I do . . ." Logan was interrupted by the bell. Class was about to begin. "Have you talked to Coach?" he asked.

"No," said Malik. "I wouldn't know what to say. Have you?"

"Yeah," said Logan. "He's pretty mad."

"I heard the school's already gotten a new coach," said Hudefa.

Daniel snorted in disgust. "Who could they find on such short notice? Any coach sitting around without a team this late in the season can't be any good. I don't want to play for someone who's got no idea what he's doing."

"Gentlemen in the back," said the substitute teacher. "Quiet down please. It's time to get started."

Logan rolled his eyes and whispered to Malik, "We'll talk more later."

***

Malik met up with Logan again at lunch. They always shared a small table in the corner.

"Big news," said Logan between mouthfuls of spaghetti. "We're going to quit the team."

"Who's going to quit?" asked Malik.

"All of us," said Logan excitedly. "Me, Daniel, and Hudefa." He wiped his face with a napkin. "We're doing it as a protest. To show our support for Coach. If they want to suspend us for the next five games, we might as well just quit."

Malik didn't know what to say. *Is Logan serious?* he wondered. They couldn't quit. This was their senior season, their last chance to play together and their last chance to get that state championship they'd been shooting for. A five-game suspension wasn't the end of the world. Logan had to be joking.

"You should do it too," Logan said. "You said yourself that we need to find a way to get Coach back. You're the best player on the team, and our captain. If you quit that would send a huge message to Mr. Wiggins and the rest of the administration. That might make them change their minds."

Malik shook his head. "I'm not quitting."

"Why not?" asked Logan. "Don't you support Coach?"

"Of course I do," he said. "But quitting isn't going to help anything."

Logan shook his head. "I thought you wanted to support Coach. Quitting is better than playing for some new guy we don't know and who doesn't know us. If you stay on the team, it's like you think what happened to Coach is okay. It's like you agree with him getting fired."

"You know I don't think what they did to Coach is okay." Malik couldn't believe what Logan was telling him. "I don't like this any more than you do, but I have to think about my future. You know that if I quit I'll lose my scholarship offers. My chance to play in college will be over. I'll lose everything I've worked for."

"Typical." Logan scoffed. "Once again Malik is thinking only about Malik."

"That's not true," Malik argued. Logan was really starting to annoy him. "I just don't think quitting is our only option."

"If you don't join us and quit, then you're just being selfish."

Malik shook his head. "You can call me selfish if you want, but I have the rest of my life to consider."

"Whatever," said Logan. He picked up his tray. "Daniel won't be too happy when I tell him."

Malik felt his face turn an angry red. "You think I care how Daniel feels?"

"He says you're a traitor," said Logan, standing up. "Daniel thinks you don't really care about Coach and that you're just putting on a big act to make it look like you do."

Malik tried not to show his shock. "And what about you?" he asked. "What do you think?"

"I'm not sure what to think anymore." Logan turned and walked away.

Malik was angry. He wanted to support Logan and Coach Washington, but Logan was making that impossible. *There has to be another way to get Coach back without quitting*, he thought. *Coach deserves my help, but he wouldn't tell me to quit the team.* He sat motionless, gazing blindly across the cafeteria. Logan had forced him into a no-win situation, and he had absolutely no idea what to do next.

AFTER school, Malik changed into his practice uniform and made his way to the soccer field. He couldn't get himself cheered up. Three experienced teammates were off the team, he was becoming more and more concerned they'd never get Coach back, and he couldn't stop thinking about Logan wanting him to quit.

Moments later Malik stood on the field with his teammates, gathered in front of the new coach. "My name is Coach Howard," the guy said. Coach Howard was young—a lot younger than Coach Washington. "I know this isn't easy for any of us. I understand that. But we're going to move on from what happened and make the most of the rest of this season. I promise you I will do my best as your coach. All I ask is that you give me your best as players."

The guys looked at each other. No one spoke up.

"So which one of you is Malik?" asked Coach Howard. "Where's our captain?"

All eyes went to him. Malik tentatively raised his hand.

"You want to get us warmed up?" asked Coach Howard.

Malik shrugged.

"Or I can do it if you want," said Coach.

Malik looked away. "Go ahead."

Coach Howard nodded. "Okay then. Guys!" he shouted. "Three laps then meet in the center!"

The players raced toward the nearest goal then ran three times around the outside of the field. Malik ran more slowly than normal. He just couldn't muster the desire to perform for Coach Howard. His real coach was Coach Washington, not this amateur. Besides, moving on and surrendering his loyalty over to Coach Howard without him earning it first felt as if he was turning his back on Coach Washington.

A couple minutes later, the team stood huffing and puffing around the circle. "Partner up!" Coach shouted. "You guys know how to do forward swings?" Several players nodded. "Okay then, ten of them. Each leg!" Malik partnered up with Reggie, a freshman. They stood next to each other, locked arms, and did twenty high kicks together.

"Same thing," said Coach when they had finished. "But cross body this time." Malik and Reggie did the drill, keeping their arms locked but kicking their legs across their bodies instead.

"On the line!" called Coach Howard after the leg swings. "Follow what I do!" He went on to lead the team in several more warm-up and stretching drills. Many of the drills were ones the team had done before. Some of them were new. Malik kept quiet the whole time. He was not his normal, vocal self, yelling encouragement to the players like he typically did. He couldn't stop thinking about Logan and the other guys who had quit. The team would never be the same. They would never be as good. On top of that, he wanted Coach Washington back. He wanted things to return to the way they used to be.

"All right, boys. Water break!" Coach Howard called when the drills were finished. The guys jogged toward the sidelines. Malik began to follow them. "Hey, Captain!" said Coach.

Malik turned around.

"Bring it in here." Coach Howard waved him over.

Malik jogged up to him.

"How's everything?" asked Coach.

"I'm all right," said Malik.

"You sure? You're pretty quiet out there."

"It's all good," said Malik. He looked at his feet.

"Okay," said Coach. "But if you have something to say, be sure to speak up, okay?"

"Yeah," said Malik.

An awkward silence followed. "I understand you must be upset about what happened to Coach Washington and your teammates."

Malik shrugged.

"I want you to know that I'm here for you," said Coach. "I want us to get along. And for this to work, I'm depending on you to lead the team through this difficult situation. You think you can do that?"

Malik looked at him at nodded, but he said nothing. Coach Howard didn't seem like a bad guy, but Malik couldn't force himself to trust him. *He's only here because another coach got fired,* thought Malik. *He doesn't deserve this job.*

"Good," said Coach Howard. "All right then. Go get some water."

Malik headed for the sidelines.

After the break, Coach Howard divided them into two teams for a scrimmage. It was green versus red. "Play your hardest! I want to see what you've got! Impress me out there!"

Malik scoffed. *I couldn't care less about impressing this guy,* he thought as he put on his red vest.

The scrimmage began. Malik's team got the ball first. His teammate, Reggie, controlled the kickoff then passed the ball wide to Omar on the right. Malik jogged slowly up the left side. Omar dribbled forward then passed it back to the middle. "Let's hear you out there!" shouted Coach Howard. "Talk to each other!"

"Up!" yelled Reggie who was streaking toward the box. He received the pass and immediately looked left. Malik wasn't open. He shook his head. *Go the other way,* he thought. *I don't want the ball.* But Reggie passed it to him anyway. Malik made a half-hearted attempt to retrieve the ball, but it was stolen away by Theo, a defender on the other team. Theo then raced past Malik in the opposite direction.

Three passes later, Antonio from the green team had the ball in front of the red team's goal. He shook off the only defender still in front of him then kicked a solid shot past the fingertips of the goalie and into the net. He and his teammates celebrated.

"Come on red team!" shouted Coach. "Get it together! Stay positive and help each other out there!"

But things did not get any better for Malik and his teammates over the next several minutes. The green team maintained control of the ball, pressing forward and keeping the red team on its heels. Malik noticed his teammates kept looking at him. He figured they were expecting his leadership. *Quit waiting for me to tell you what to do*, he thought. *Don't you all realize this pointless scrimmage means nothing to me?*

Theo finally lofted a cross into the box. Red team defenders were too late to react and Antonio blasted a header into the back of the net.

"Red team, you have to find someone to mark!" yelled Coach. "Green team, excellent play!"

Things went from bad to worse for the red team. They were defeated 6–0 and had to run extra sprints when it was over. Malik ran his sprints with little emotion. He wasn't angry. He wasn't fired up. He was just numb.

MALIK was still in a funk Friday morning at school. It didn't help that he arrived late to first period and found out Coach Howard had taken over all of Coach Washington's classes.

"Nice of you to join us," said Coach as Malik walked into first period history class.

Logan and Daniel were sitting together in the back row. Malik shuffled across the room with his head down and walked toward the only available seat—a chair in front of Daniel. "Seat's taken," he said.

"By who?" Malik asked.

"Malik," said Coach Howard. "Please have a seat."

Malik turned his back to Daniel and sat down. He could hear Daniel and Logan snickering behind him. *Really?* he thought. *So that's how it's going to be now?* It didn't surprise him that Daniel was behaving like a child, but why was Logan sinking to his level?

"Can you believe we got stuck with Howard?" Logan asked Daniel. He was talking loudly. Loudly enough for Malik, and probably Coach Howard, to hear him.

"This guy's the worst," said Daniel, speaking loudly too.

Malik remained silent. He had no love for Coach Howard, but Daniel and Logan were crossing the line.

"Gentlemen," said Coach Howard. "I need your attention up here."

Logan and Daniel chuckled under their breath.

"As I was saying," said Coach Howard. "I love history and it's my goal to make you love it too. History is our past. Your past and mine. And like Winston Churchill famously said, 'Those who fail to learn from history will be doomed to repeat it.' That's the quote I live by."

"I'm doomed to repeat this class," said Daniel. A couple girls in the next row over giggled.

"Wish we could quit history like we quit soccer," whispered Daniel.

Malik turned around. "Would you guys be quiet?"

"What?" asked Logan. "You like this guy or something?"

"I told you," Daniel said to Logan. "He doesn't care about Coach losing his job. He's already buddies with Howard."

"We're not buddies," insisted Malik.

"Boys," said Coach Howard. "I've warned you once already. Keep your comments to yourself or there will be consequences."

"Ooh, tough guy!" said Daniel at full volume.

"We're so scared," said Logan.

Coach Howard gritted his teeth. It was clear he'd had enough. "When you're in my class, you respect me and my rules. If you're not willing to do those things, Mr. Wiggins is a phone call away."

Daniel suddenly stood up, knocking his chair noisily to the side. He puffed out his chest and stared down Coach Howard. "This class is the worst."

The classroom went dead quiet. Daniel stormed toward the door. "Logan, let's go."

Don't do it, Logan, thought Malik. But Logan got up and walked over to Daniel at the doorway then turned back around. "Malik, you coming?" he asked.

"What?" said Malik. "No, I am not coming with you."

"See what I mean?" said Daniel. "Malik only cares about himself. Come on."

"You two leave and this becomes a much bigger issue," warned Coach Howard.

"Who cares?" said Daniel, flinging open the door. He and Logan disappeared into the hallway.

Malik slumped down in his chair. He wondered if this situation could possibly get any worse.

SKIP *practice and meet me at Oak Hill Park. I have a new idea to get Coach his job back.* The text was from Logan. Malik read it in the hallway after seventh period.

Malik didn't know what to think. *Logan hasn't been much of a friend lately, and now he wants to hang out?* But Malik was intrigued that Logan had come up with a plan to bring Coach back. He wanted to hear what it was.

Malik never missed practice, but what was the harm of missing it just once? He would survive, and so would the team. He could tell Coach Howard he'd gotten sick or something. And if skipping practice meant helping Coach Washington, it would definitely be worth it.

***

"I told you he'd come," said Logan as Malik walked up to them at Oak Hill Park. Logan and Daniel were standing together. They both wore sly grins on their faces. "I told you he'd listen to me."

"Good work," said Daniel, giving Logan a fist pump.

"What's going on?" said Malik. "Logan, you didn't tell me Daniel was going to be here." Malik immediately regretted skipping practice.

Logan shrugged his shoulders. "I didn't think you'd care."

Malik glanced around the park, trying to swallow his irritation. "So what's this plan, Logan?" he asked. "How are we going to get Coach his job back?"

Daniel snorted with laughter.

Logan said nothing.

"What's so funny?" Malik asked.

Logan paused. "There is no plan," he said.

Malik was confused. "So why'd you invite me here?"

"To get you to tell the truth," said Logan.

"To get you to admit that you cheated like the rest of us."

Malik stared at Logan as he tried to process what his friend had said. "What are you talking about?"

"You cheated," said Logan. "I cheated. We all cheated. You just didn't get caught."

"*What?*"

Logan shrugged. "Daniel told me today that he saw Coach give you the answer keys last week."

"Wait a minute." Malik's brain was still struggling to catch up with Logan's words. "You mean you guys *did* cheat? You told me before that you didn't."

"Yes, I technically cheated," said Logan. "And so did you."

"No I didn't." Malik was so stunned by Logan's confession, he almost forgot about Coach Washington. "So—Coach really did help you cheat? It's true?"

"You know it's true," said Logan. "He helped you too."

Malik buried his head in his hands.

Everything he'd thought about Coach and everything he'd believed about the cheating scandal had been wrong. His brain couldn't calculate it all. "But I didn't cheat!" he shouted.

"Man, let's get out of here," Daniel said to Logan, shaking his head.

"Mr. Wiggins is going to find out you cheated just like we did," said Logan. "And when he does, you'll wish you had confessed when you had the chance." He turned and followed Daniel.

Malik watched them walk away. He was in utter shock. A few minutes ago he had been excited—motivated to help his friend and to help the coach he'd always loved. But as he stood there, alone in the park, he was devastated. He best friend had lied to him, and Coach Washington had cheated after all.

***

Malik spent the weekend feeling as if his insides were twisted up like a pretzel. *How could Coach have helped the guys cheat? How could he have done that to me? And to the team? He ruined*

*everything. I wonder if he cheated in other ways
too. Or told other lies?* Malik's trust in Coach
Washington had been completely shattered.

He was also furious at Logan. *Why is Logan
stabbing me in the back?* Malik wondered. *Did he
really believe I cheated too?*

All the drama made his head hurt. By
Monday morning he was tired of thinking
about it. He realized there was only one thing
that might make him feel better and take his
mind off the whole scandal. He needed to get
back on the soccer field.

Before school started he walked directly to
Coach Howard's office. It was time to apologize
for the way he'd been acting. It was time to act
like a captain again. He knocked on the door.

"Yes?" Coach Howard turned and smiled
at him. "Malik. Come on in." Malik slowly
opened the door and stepped inside the office.
"Have a seat." He sat down on an old, springy
chair across from Coach Howard.

Coach Howard smiled. "How's it going?"

"It's good." Malik didn't know where to
start. "Sorry if I'm interrupting anything."

"Not at all," he said. He looked at a stack of papers on his desk. "I've just been correcting some history quizzes."

Coach Howard's face turned serious. "We missed you on Friday."

"Yeah," said Malik. "I know. That's why I'm here. I wanted to let you know that it won't happen again, I promise."

"Good," said Coach. "I was getting worried you might follow the other guys and quit."

"No," said Malik. "I'm not quitting."

"Good," said Coach Howard. "That's a relief."

Malik nodded. He looked toward the door and then back at Coach Howard. It was time to make things right.

"I also wanted to say I'm sorry for how I've acted," said Malik. "I haven't given you a chance and I definitely haven't been behaving like a captain. That's all going to change. Immediately."

"I'm glad to hear that," said Coach.

"Will you accept my apology?" Malik stuck out his hand.

"Of course." Coach Howard gave Malik a hearty handshake.

Malik let go then leaned back in his chair. A long moment of silence filled the room.

"Is there something else?" asked Coach.

"Is it true?" Malik eventually stammered. His throat suddenly dried up. "Did Coach Washington really help those other guys cheat?"

Coach Howard scratched his forehead. He nodded. "I'm afraid so."

Malik lowered his head so Coach Howard wouldn't see his eyes watering.

"I know this can't be easy for you," said Coach Howard. "I want you to know I'm here for you. For anything you need."

Malik rubbed the tears away. "Thanks. I appreciate that." He got up and walked to the door. "See you in history class."

Malik left the office and stepped into the hallway. *Coach Washington really did it*, he thought. *There's no doubt about it.* It was hard to hear the truth, but he was relieved he could finally stop wondering.

But apologizing to Coach Howard and learning the truth about Coach Washington didn't make things any better with Logan. That was a whole different challenge that he had no idea how to solve.

AFTER school, Malik made his way to practice. He was one of the first players to arrive, ready to be a vocal leader on and off the field once again.

Coach led the team in stretches and sprints to start the practice. "Looking good Omar!" Malik shouted. "Faster Reggie! You can do it!" he called out in encouragement.

Malik also pushed himself physically. He ran out every sprint. He gave 100 percent during every drill. And he out-performed every player. He wanted to show Coach Howard that he meant what he had said that morning in his office: he was ready to get back to playing soccer and being a leader.

"Nice effort, Malik!" shouted Coach. "He's your target, everyone. During sprints and warm-ups your goal should be to hang with him." The players stood around, bent over, each trying to catch his breath.

"All right. Line up for tic-tac-toe!" shouted Coach. The players cheered. Malik looked around. He had no idea what was going on.

Coach set up nine small, orange cones about six feet apart in a grid pattern. Meanwhile, Malik walked over to Reggie. "What's going on?"

"It's tic-tac-toe," said Reggie. "We did it on Friday. It's awesome."

"Two teams!" shouted Coach. "Split yourselves up behind the yellow cones!"

About twenty feet away from the red cones were two yellow cones. Malik's teammates ran toward them, getting into position behind the yellow cones. Half of the team lined up behind one of the yellow cones, half lined up behind the other. Malik jogged over to join them.

"Malik! Over here!" It was Reggie, waving at him from his line.

"No, come to our team!" Omar was yelling at him from the other line.

Malik smiled and ran to the back of Reggie's line.

"You need a crash course in how the game works, Malik?" asked Coach.

"Nah, I'll figure it out."

The two players in the front of each line raced toward the nine orange cones. Malik watched to make sure he knew what to do when it was his turn. They held warm-up vests in their hands. Malik's teammate, Antonio, held a red vest. Theo held a green. When the two of them got to the cones, they each quickly placed their vest on top of one of the orange cones in the grid then sprinted back to the end of the line. The next players in line did the same thing, running to place their vest strategically onto a cone.

Malik got it. Each team was trying to get their vests onto three cones in a row in the grid of nine cones. It was just like tic-tac-toe. *Cool game*, he thought. *It forces you to strategize, think quickly on your feet, and it's fun too. Nice job, Coach.*

The third players in line raced to dump their vests onto cones, but neither team was able to get three in a row. The other players cheered on their teammates.

The next players in line didn't have vests. Instead they ran to the grid and picked up one of their team's vests that had already been placed onto the grid. Then they moved the vest to another cone, again trying for three in a row.

"Let's go red!" shouted Reggie.

"Come on green!" yelled Omar.

Malik looked around and laughed. His teammates were having a great time. He waited and watched. Reggie was next, then he'd be up.

Reggie got the hand-off from the player in front of him, then he sprinted toward the orange cones. He danced around, not quite sure which vest to pick up. Ben, his opponent from green was doing the same thing.

"Come on fellas!" yelled Coach. "This isn't the prom!" Everyone laughed.

Reggie grabbed the vest from one of the corners then dumped it onto a different cone. He couldn't get three in a row. Neither could Ben.

Reggie then raced back to Malik. Malik slapped his hand and ran to the grid. Omar, from green, was right beside him.

Malik sprinted to the grid of cones and froze. He didn't know which vest to pick up. He couldn't see a way to get three in a row. He shuffled around on his feet, wanting to make a move but unsure exactly which vest was the right one to grab.

"Nice dance steps!" yelled Coach. The guys laughed.

Malik smiled and shook his head. He couldn't think straight. He was feeling the pressure.

Suddenly Omar made a move. He reached for the green vest on the middle cone, picked it up and quickly tossed it on top of one of the corner cones. "Got it!" yelled Omar. Sure enough, Omar had gotten three in a row.

The green team celebrated. Omar stepped toward Malik, his hand in the air. Malik gave him a high five. "Good game," said Omar.

"You too." Malik said.

"One more?" yelled Coach.

Everyone on both teams cheered and immediately got into positions again behind the yellow cones.

Malik looked at Coach Howard. Coach gave him a smile and a thumbs-up. Malik smiled back. Just like that, soccer had suddenly become fun again.

THE next day Malik and the team were back
on the field, this time playing in their first
game under Coach Howard. The Gators were
taking on the Ponies from Eastlake.

Coach Howard gathered the players around
him before the game and announced the
starting lineup. It included one sophomore and
two freshmen, guys who hadn't seen significant
playing time during previous games. Reggie
and Omar would be starting defenders. They
were playing in place of Logan and Daniel.

Having two new players on defense—two
guys with very limited experience—was not
the ideal situation. But Coach Howard had no
choice since three of his top players were no
longer on the team. Malik worried the team

would be extra vulnerable to allowing goals, which meant he would have to play his absolute best on offense to make up the difference.

"Let's have some fun out there," said Coach Howard in his pregame speech. "We're starting fresh with some new players. And a new coach of course." Some of the players chuckled. "But I believe in you guys. Let's go out there and see what we're made of." He turned to Malik. "Any words, Captain?"

Malik cleared his throat and looked at the players. The drama of the past few days still hung like a cloud over the team, but they had to move forward. "Give it everything you've got, guys," he said. "We can do this." He stepped into the middle of the circle and put his arm into the air. The other guys did the same and crowded together. "One, two, three!" shouted Malik.

"Gators!" the team yelled in unison.

The Gators held their own for the first fifteen minutes of the game. Malik played well, setting up other players for several scoring opportunities. The Ponies knew about Malik's talent so they were running multiple guys on him. Malik needed to look for assists rather than goals because he didn't have the space to get himself clear for quality shots.

Unfortunately, none of Malik's passes resulted in goals. The closest the Gators got was a long shot from Reggie that went over the hands of the Ponies' goalie but bounced hard off the crossbar. Reggie had missed a goal by just a few inches.

Then the game took a turn. Something seemed to click for the Ponies and they took control, keeping the ball for much of the half and launching a barrage of shots at the Gators' goal. Reggie, Omar, and the other Gators defenders became the victims.

When the Gators finally got the ball, Theo dribbled it into the far corner. While Malik and his teammates were setting up for a scoring chance, Omar and the other defenders drifted close to the box. They were playing too far forward in the Ponies end. *You're giving them an easy chance at a counterattack*, he thought. "Omar, back up!" Malik yelled.

Reggie was alone near the center circle. When a Ponies player intercepted a pass and kicked it to the player Reggie was marking, no one else was back to help him. The player took off with the ball, sprinted past Reggie, and raced toward the Gators' goal.

Reggie chased him down. He played him tight and stayed with him as the Ponies forward dribbled toward the goal. But defending a guy one-on-one across half of the field was just too much of a challenge. When the Ponies player got close to the goal, he moved to the left, stopped the ball, then shifted to the right. Reggie couldn't stop his momentum and he sprinted wildly past the ball, setting up an easy scoring chance. The Ponies player set himself, then drilled the shot past the diving goalie and into the net.

Minutes later, the Ponies controlled the ball again. As a player from the Ponies dribbled into the zone along the left sideline, Reggie and Omar were marking two other players hovering in front of the goal. A pass came toward the player Reggie was defending.

Instead of standing his ground when the player received the pass and forcing him to make a move, Reggie lunged forward, allowing the player to dribble easily past him.

The player who had gotten around Reggie dribbled toward the goal but then lost control, pushing the ball too far forward. Omar was there. The ball came straight at him. It looked like it would be an easy defensive stop. But instead of trapping the ball or clearing it out of the zone, he misplayed it and kicked the ball right back to the forward who had just lost it. The player blasted the ball into the goal.

Malik dropped his head in frustration. *That goal wouldn't have happened if Logan was on the field*, he thought. *He would have defended the ball and cleared it out.*

He looked to the sidelines. Coach Howard was clapping. "That's all right, guys!" he shouted. "Let's get one back now!"

Malik was impressed by his reaction. Coach Howard was upbeat even though his players had just made some basic mistakes. Coach Washington would've sent the guys to the bench and given them a real tongue lashing—he had even been known to make some players cry. Seeing Coach Howard yelling encouragement to his players, despite some pretty awful plays, was something Malik wasn't used to. But he noticed that the guys were responding to it. *They're staying positive*, he thought as he watched his teammates sprint back to their positions. *They're not hanging their heads or getting down on themselves even though we're down by two.*

The remaining minutes of the first half ticked off the clock. The Ponies kept control of the ball but thankfully failed to score again. When the referee blew his whistle, the Gators were trailing the Ponies 2–0.

THE players took a seat on the bench at halftime. Coach Howard paced back and forth in front of them. "We made enough mistakes out there for an entire game, am I right?" He smiled.

The players nodded. "Then you're not allowed to make any more." He laughed. "Just joking of course. Mistakes are part of the game, but let's try to sharpen things up. Do the little things and the goals will take care of themselves."

"Let's pick it up, guys!" Malik said. "We can play a lot better than this."

Coach nodded his head. "You're great players, all of you. Like I said before the game, I believe in this team." He walked along the bench. "One half of one game does not define us. What defines us is what we do after we get down 2–0. That's when we prove who we are. That's when we prove we're champions."

Again, Malik was impressed. Coach Howard kept things positive and treated the players with respect. *He really seems to care about us*, Malik thought. Malik just hoped it would translate into improved play.

Halftime ended and the players jogged onto the field.

"Let's go boys!" Malik clapped his hands. "Play smart! Play hard! Leave everything on the field!"

Immediately it was obvious that the Gators were a different team than the one from the first half. Their defense tightened things up and closed all the gaps. The Ponies continued to try to advance the ball toward the Gators' goal, but time after time Omar intercepted their passes or tackled the ball away. The Ponies could get absolutely no momentum going.

Great play!" shouted Malik after Omar stood his ground and forced a Ponies player to dribble the ball out of bounds.

Omar tossed the ball to Reggie, who then dribbled hard along the left side toward the Ponies' goal. Malik suddenly got free. Reggie spotted him and led him with a nearly perfect pass. Malik sprinted ahead of his closest defender, closing on the ball. Unfortunately, the goalie got there a split second before Malik could. He slid sideways and scooped up the ball. Malik jumped over him, making sure not to run into the goalie. He then gave a thumbs-up to Reggie. "Awesome pass!" he yelled. Reggie returned the thumbs-up.

After that, the Gators dominated control of the ball. They held the ball in the Ponies' end throughout the second half and kept their opponent off the scoreboard. Their biggest challenge became the clock. As minutes ticked by, Malik realized getting two goals in the time that remained was going to be tough, but he wanted to make sure his teammates kept pressing and kept playing their best until the final whistle.

"Let's go, guys!" he shouted after one of the Ponies tackled the ball away from him and knocked it out of bounds. Reggie ran up for the throw-in. Malik sprinted toward the goal. "Keep up the intensity! Play to the end!"

Malik settled into a spot about ten yards in front of the box. The Ponies' goalie guarded the goal behind him. Reggie threw the ball to Omar, near the center circle. Malik made a move. "Open!" he yelled. Omar passed him the ball.

Malik controlled it then sent it back wide to Reggie along the right. Reggie dribbled forward, putting pressure on the defender in front of him. Malik positioned himself in the box.

Reggie suddenly stopped, controlling the ball with his foot. He then made a move that blew Malik away. He shifted the ball to his right foot, then his left, and then back again. His defender was on his heels. Reggie then flicked the ball into the air and over the shoulder of the defender. He sprinted past, regained the ball and sent a vicious cross toward the goal.

Malik was so impressed by the move, he almost forgot to react. But he quickly snapped to attention, got free, and raced to meet the ball. He trapped it, turned, and fired a low shot under the diving arms of the goalie. His kick took him to the ground. He landed on his back and watched the ball sail beautifully into the net.

His teammates piled on top of him. It was hard for Malik to remember a goal that had felt better. He got to his feet and accepted hugs and high fives from his teammates. Reggie was last on the scene. "That move!" said Malik. "Where did that come from?"

"I've been practicing," said Reggie.

"Apparently you have." Malik laughed, pushing Reggie playfully toward the middle of the field.

Malik looked to the sidelines. "Awesome play!' shouted Coach Howard. "That's how you do it!"

The game ended just minutes later. The Ponies held on for a 2–1 win, but Malik felt like he and the guys had achieved something of a victory. They had held their ground in the second half, scoring one goal and keeping the Ponies from adding to their total. He was proud of his teammates, and excited for the rest of the season.

As he was congratulating the guys on a hard-fought game, he glanced up at the bleachers. He was surprised to see Logan. He was by himself, walking down the steps and toward the exit. *I wonder what he's doing here*, Malik thought. *Does he want to be back on the team?*

MALIK biked to school the following day, and he ran into Omar and Reggie at the bike rack in front of the school.

"I'm still thinking about that move you put on the player from Eastlake yesterday," Malik said to Reggie as he knelt down to lock up his bike. "It was brilliant. Then the pass to me. Wow."

"Thanks," Reggie mumbled.

"Are you blushing?" Malik laughed.

"Reggie's not much into bragging," said Omar.

"That's good," said Malik standing up. "I like that. But, Reggie, you can still be proud of your talent. And don't be afraid to show it off on the field." He patted Reggie on the shoulder. "If you keep making moves like that, I think we'll need to talk to Coach about putting you up front in a forward position. I see a lot of goals in your future."

"That would be cool," said Reggie. "But for now I'm totally fine playing defense."

"Whatever helps the team, am I right?" said Omar.

"That's what I like to hear." Malik slung his backpack over his shoulders. "Well, I've got to get to class. See you at practice."

Malik headed inside. As he started up the staircase, somebody jogged up alongside him. It was Logan.

"I saw your game yesterday," said Logan.

Malik kept walking. "Yeah? What about it?"

"You guys got clobbered," laughed Logan. "By Eastlake. How embarrassing."

"I wouldn't say we got clobbered," said Malik. "We played a solid second half and improved a lot as the game went on." They continued to climb the stairs.

"That's great," said Logan, sneering. "Improvement is good. I'd rather have the win."

Malik stopped at the top of the stairs. "You have something to say to me?" he asked, annoyed at Logan's comments.

"As a matter of fact, I do," said Logan. "Why didn't you tell Mr. Wiggins that you cheated?"

"This again?" asked Malik. "I already told you that I didn't cheat."

"Your friends get suspended and you say nothing," said Logan. "You pretend like you weren't involved and you let us take all the heat."

"How many times do I have to tell you?" said Malik. "I swear to you, Logan, I never cheated. Frankly, it kind of hurts that you don't believe me. First you tell me you didn't cheat when you really did. Now you won't believe me when I tell you I didn't. I thought we trusted each other. I thought we were friends."

Logan seemed unable to accept what Malik was telling him. "But Daniel saw you. He saw Coach give you the answer key."

Malik shook his head. "Daniel's lying," said Malik. "Coach never gave me any answers.

Daniel's just saying that because he doesn't like me and he's mad about being suspended. He's trying to drag me down with him."

"Yeah but . . ."

Malik interrupted. "Logan, you and I have been best friends forever. I wouldn't lie to you. Really, who are you going to believe? Daniel or me?"

Logan leaned against the railing, his eyebrows scrunched together in thought. After a moment he pulled out his phone. "I need to get going. I've got to talk to Daniel."

"You believe me, right?" asked Malik.

"I'm not sure." Logan walked away.

Malik let out a frustrated sigh. He wondered if he could find a way to convince Logan that he was telling the truth.

MALIK hoped to talk to Logan during history class, but Logan was sitting with Daniel. Malik knew he'd never have any luck changing Logan's mind as long as Daniel was around. He sat in the front row instead. He then tried catching Logan at lunch, but he was too late—Logan and Daniel had already sat down together. His conversation with Logan would have to wait.

After the final bell, Malik went to the locker room to get ready for practice. His teammates were upbeat. "I'm going to school you in sprints today," said Omar.

"Is that right?" Malik smiled.

"Your days of domination are over!" said Omar dramatically.

"Keep dreaming." Reggie laughed. "Omar, you've got no speed."

"You watch," said Omar. "Today's the day."

"Malik." He turned around. It was Coach Howard. He was standing at the far end of the locker room. His face was completely blank. "Can I see you for a minute?" he asked.

Malik nodded. "Of course." He stood and followed Coach Howard to his office, wondering what was up. When he got to the door, it was clear—Mr. Wiggins, was sitting in one of the office chairs. *This must have something to do with the whole cheating mess*, he thought, his heart sinking.

Mr. Wiggins stood up.

"Malik, please have a seat." Mr. Wiggins motioned to the chair next to him. Coach Howard sat down behind his desk. "I want to respect Coach Howard's time, so I'm going to get right to it," said Mr. Wiggins after they were all seated. "Someone came to me and reported that you were involved in the cheating situation that caused Coach Washington to lose his job."

Malik immediately became angry. He felt his body get warm, his face turn red. *I bet it was Daniel*, he thought. Suddenly his mind flashed back to the conversation this morning with Logan. *But what if it was Logan? He wouldn't sink to that level, would he?*

"I want to give you the opportunity to tell your side of the story," said Mr. Wiggins.

Malik was enraged. He was sick of this whole cheating thing. He wanted to get outside to practice for the game tomorrow against Ridgemont. This was all a giant waste of time. "There is no story!" His voice was loud and aggressive. "I didn't do anything."

"Take it easy, Malik," said Mr. Wiggins. "I'm not accusing you of anything."

"It sounds like you are," said Malik. He tried his best to calm down.

"I just wanted to hear it straight from you," said Mr. Wiggins. "To give you a chance to confess if you had any part in this."

"I didn't," said Malik.

Mr. Wiggins gave him a serious look and leaned in closer. "You're sure there's absolutely nothing you want to tell me?"

"Nothing," said Malik. "Until Coach Washington got fired, I never had any clue that he was helping anyone cheat. He definitely wasn't helping *me*. I mean, you can compare my grade in history this year to the rest of my high school transcript. I've always done fine in my history classes, and my other teachers weren't helping anyone cheat."

"Mr. Wiggins," said Coach Howard. "I believe Malik. If he said he didn't cheat, he didn't cheat. I've gotten to know Malik and there's absolutely nothing about the young man that would lead me to believe he's trying to deceive us. That's not who he is."

"I agree with you, Coach," said Mr. Wiggins. "Frankly, I found it odd that the person waited until now to come to me." He got up from his chair. "I believe I'm done here."

"Perfect." Coach stood up. "Malik, you can go out on the field."

"Thanks for your time, son," said Mr. Wiggins.

Malik got up and stepped into the hallway.

He looked back into the office. Coach Howard gave him a nod.

Coach had his back. It felt good. He knew Coach was on his side, that if he needed him he would be there.

But what about Logan? he thought. *Was he the one who reported me to Mr. Wiggins? Did he try to sell me out?*

THE next day the Gators took to the road to square off against the Ridgemont Raiders. Malik could hardly wait to take the field. Practice the day before had been their best one yet. The new players seemed to finally be clicking with the more experienced guys, and enthusiasm was never higher since Coach Howard had taken over.

The players changed in the Raiders locker room then headed to the field. Malik joked around with Reggie and Omar during the long walk. When they entered through the gate to the field, he was surprised to see Logan standing on the other side of the fence.

He stepped in front of Malik. The look on his face was somber. "Can I talk to you?"

"What are you doing here?" asked Malik. He stopped. The rest of the guys jogged onto the field.

"We need to talk," said Logan.

"Can it wait?" asked Malik. He had wanted to talk to Logan during school, but now he had a game to play.

Logan grabbed Malik's arm. "It will just take a minute." Malik looked down at Logan's hand.

"Sorry." Logan let go of Malik. "But I need to tell you something."

Malik was annoyed. If Logan was there to accuse him of cheating again, he wanted nothing to do with it.

"It wasn't me who went to Mr. Wiggins," said Logan.

Malik just looked at him. He didn't know if he could believe Logan.

"I was planning to, before I talked to you yesterday morning," said Logan. "I believed Daniel, and I was mad at you for not telling the truth. But then I finally realized Daniel was the one lying."

"What made you realize that?" said Malik.

"Because you're my friend," said Logan simply. "And you never lie. I trust you, and I should've trusted you all along. I'm really sorry."

"Why did it take you so long to believe me?" asked Malik. He was still hurt that Logan hadn't trusted him from the beginning.

"Because Daniel was always in my face," said Logan. "He was saying that you're fake and that you aren't really my friend. And after the suspension, it felt like us against the world. But when you and I talked yesterday morning and I thought of everything we've been through together, I realized that Daniel was wrong and that you would never stab me in the back. You've always been there for me."

Malik wanted to accept the apology, but he needed to hear something else first. "Logan, why did you cheat?"

Logan looked at the ground. "Coach Washington didn't want us to fail history— that would've made us ineligible to play. So he changed our answers on some tests to make sure we passed."

Malik sighed. "That was really stupid," he said.

"I know," said Logan. "But I only did it a couple times. That doesn't make it right, I get that. But I did it because I was freaked out I was going to fail and get kicked off the team. And I guess I thought if Coach was doing it, that it was okay."

"I still can't believe Coach Washington cheated like that." Malik shook his head. "I really respected him."

"I know," said Logan. "I'm sorry this whole thing happened."

"It's not your fault Coach did what he did," said Malik. He put his hand on Logan's shoulder. "Coach is a grown man. He made a dumb choice. Nobody forced him to change your answers. He's the one who should feel bad for what happened to you guys. And listen, if you've been having that much trouble in history, I can helped you study for the tests."

Logan looked away. "Thanks, man." He wiped his eyes with the side of his arm. "I talked to Coach Howard."

"Yeah?" said Malik.

"He's taking me back," said Logan. "I have to serve my suspension, but in a couple of weeks I'll be back on the team."

"That's great news," said Malik.

Logan nodded. "I know. It is."

Malik smiled.

"Are we still friends?" he asked, sniffing in through his nose.

"Of course." Malik reached out and gave Logan a hug. "We're friends no matter what."

"Thanks, man," said Logan. After a few seconds he let go of Malik. "You've got a game to play."

"Right," said Malik.

"Then get out there." He shoved Malik toward the field.

Malik laughed then ran to join his teammates.

***

The players gathered around Coach Howard along the sidelines. It was just five minutes to game time. "If you play like you did in the second half of the last game or like you did in practice yesterday, we have nothing to worry about," said Coach. "Play your game. Remember all the things we worked on in practice and the score will take care of itself." He looked at Malik. "Captain?"

Malik stepped in front of the team. He stood without talking, dramatically looking from player to player. He then cracked a huge smile. "Who's ready to do this this?" he shouted.

The team shouted back. "We are!"

"Who's ready to take it to the Raiders?"

"We are!"

"And who's ready to win this game?" Malik yelled.

"We are!"

Malik paced in front of the guys. "Then go out on that field and play every second like it's your last. Do everything Coach Howard has taught us. Coach has shown us he's here to win. That he cares about us. That he's one of us. Let's let him know we feel the same way. Play smart. Play aggressive. And most of all . . . let's show those Raiders that you don't mess with

the Gators!" He reached his arm into the air.
"Bring it in here!"

His teammates crowded around him. Malik
screamed. "One, two, three!"

"Gators!"

THE Gators started strong. In the game's first ten minutes they controlled much of the play, keeping the ball in the Raiders' end most of the time. Whenever the Raiders did get the ball across the centerline, Reggie or Omar was there to sweep it out and get it back on the foot of a Gators forward.

Malik felt a mix of emotions. He was optimistic for the team's future, relieved things were back to normal with Logan, and truly excited to be playing for Coach Howard.

Still, with all that, he was nervous.

Especially because three men in tracksuits were sitting in the bleachers. One was wearing the red and white colors of Georgia College. The other two were in the green and gold of

East Coast U, his dream university. Coach Howard had told Malik before the game who these men were, and why they were at the game. They were scouts. And they were there to evaluate Malik to see if he was good enough to play for them. He didn't know the scout from Georgia, but he recognized the guys from East Coast U. They were the same ones he had met when he visited the school over the summer.

The smacking sound of a soccer ball being kicked snapped Malik's attention back to the game. *There's no point worrying about the scouts,* he thought. *The best way to impress them is to forget they're here. Play your best, be a leader, and dominate on the field.*

"Open!" Malik shouted, raising his arm high. The pass came his way. Malik trapped the ball with his chest, controlled it with his feet, then dribbled forward along the right sideline. A defender from the Raiders dashed toward him. Malik stopped quickly, moved the ball from his right foot to his left, then blasted past him.

His teammates were setting up around the box. Another defender got in front of him, so Malik gave up the ball, sending it backward to Omar. He then charged forward toward the box. Omar passed the ball to Reggie, who was positioned in the center of the field, about twenty yards in front of the box.

Reggie immediately spotted Malik making his run and made the pass. Malik trapped the ball with his right foot then danced around his defender. The goalie raced over to get between Malik and the goal. Malik used the goalie's momentum to his advantage. He faked a shot to the right. The goalie had no choice but to dive and go for the block. That left the goal wide open. Malik changed direction, took two steps forward and buried the ball in the back of the net. The Gators had an early 1–0 lead.

Malik's teammates mobbed around him. He savored the moment. There was hardly any feeling better than scoring a goal.

"Great play!" shouted Malik. He then singled out Reggie and Omar. "Excellent patience, guys. Good job letting the play develop."

For most of the half, the Gators controlled the play, keeping pressure on the Raiders defenders and putting several more shots on goal. But they didn't manage to put another ball into the net. The score remained 1–0 with just a couple minutes remaining before halftime.

"Keep up the intensity!" shouted Malik after the ball drifted out of bounds. Omar was there for the throw-in. "Stay focused and don't give up!"

Omar threw the ball toward Theo. Theo tried trapping it off his chest but the ball bounced wildly away from him. A Raider jumped on it, swept it forward, and dribbled toward the Gators' goal.

As he made his way down the field, the Raiders player looked up and found a teammate sprinting up the left side. Reggie was defending him. The pass to the player was perfect, leading the streaking Raider toward the end line. Reggie was a little slow in reacting. By the time the player controlled the ball and moved toward the goal, Reggie's only play was to tackle the ball and send it over the end line. The result was a Raiders corner kick.

"Good play!" shouted Malik as the players got into position inside the box. "Good defense, Reggie. We'll take the corner. The important thing is you prevented the goal!"

One of the Raiders positioned the ball in the corner and prepared for the kick.

Players moved around. The Raiders tried to find openings. The Gators stayed locked on their opponents. Bodies pushed and bumped together. Finally, the corner kick came in. Malik watched it sail high above his head. The ball was going to land ten to fifteen feet away from him. There was nothing he could do but watch and get ready to defend after the initial attempt.

The ball headed toward Omar and the player he was defending. As it dropped, Omar tried to launch himself into the air. Unfortunately, his feet got tangled up. Instead of leaping high to defend the ball, Omar went crashing to the ground. The Raider nearest him also jumped—timing his takeoff perfectly, meeting the ball with his head, and blasting it toward the goal. The goalie for the Gators had very little time to react. He dove to his right, but it was too late. The ball sailed into the net.

The Raiders celebrated.

Malik bent over and shook his head. The Gators defense had allowed only one shot the entire half. And it had resulted in the tying goal.

THE players took a seat on the bench during halftime. The score remained deadlocked at 1–1.

Malik walked in front of the players. "We're looking good out there," he said. "We're totally dominating play. And we've put some really good shots on net. If we keep playing like that, good things will happen."

"We have to shake off that goal." Malik stepped toward Omar, who was hanging his head. Malik patted him on the shoulder. "Omar, you tripped. It happens. What you need to do now—what we all need to do—is go back out there and get a goal back."

He continued to pace the sideline in front of the guys. "But what the Raiders goal shows us is that small mistakes can result in big plays. We have to play sharp for each of the next forty-five minutes. We can't let up for even a second." He looked at Coach Howard. "Coach?"

"You're on a roll, Captain," he said, smiling. "They're all yours."

Malik nodded. "All right then, guys," he said. "Everyone up." The players gathered around him. They reached their arms together in a circle. "Let's win this thing! One, two, three!"

"Gators!" the players shouted.

The game continued. The Raiders controlled the ball early, playing with a new level of intensity. The Gators were forced back into their own zone. Three Raiders passed the ball to one another just across the centerline. Malik and his teammates played things cautiously and didn't dive in for the ball. No one wanted to make a mistake. Or make a play that was too aggressive, one that might result in a Raiders goal. The guys were willing to wait for a misplay or a safe opportunity for a steal.

But their cautious attitude cost them. One of the Raiders finally made a pass. His teammate received the ball, then immediately passed it to another Raider who was making a run toward the box. Reggie tried getting in front of the player, but he was a second too late. The third Raider received the pass, checked out the positioning of the goalie, then fired. His was a beauty. The ball bent over the outstretched hands of the Gators goalie and landed inside the top left corner of the goal, in the only spot possible for a goal.

The Raiders were suddenly ahead 2–1.

"Let's get it back!" shouted Malik as the Gators set up for the kickoff.

Reggie received the kickoff. He immediately sent the ball wide to Malik on the right sideline. Malik was hungry to get a goal to tie the game and have the rest of the half to score the winning goal. He wanted a win. Not just to impress Coach Howard or the scouts from East Coast University. He wanted the win for himself and for his teammates.

He dribbled up the sideline. His defender stayed on him, but he kept his distance, trying to keep in front of Malik.

Malik passed the ball to Theo in the middle of the field, who trapped it and sent it wide to Antonio on the left. With the Raiders defense shifting away from Malik and toward the left half of the field, he had some room to operate. He waved his arm in the air, hoping for the pass. Antonio saw him and put his whole leg into the pass. The ball sailed over the heads of the entire Raiders team and landed perfectly at Malik's feet. He secured the ball, rushed past his defender, and dribbled toward the end line. The Raiders goalie shifted over to cut off the angle. Malik knew he had to move fast or other defenders would get there soon to cover him. He shifted the ball back and forth on his feet, dodged another defender, and bolted toward the goal.

The goalie was there, but Malik spotted a low opening. The goalie was standing too upright. He seemed worried about a shot high into the corners, which left an opportunity to take the ball low. Malik took the shot, making sure to hit the ball straight on and not get under it. The ball streaked across the turf and under the left arm of the goalie. The goalie tried desperately to kick his leg out to stop the ball, but it was no use. Malik's shot was already past him and in the net.

Malik ran into the corner, grinning. His teammates ran over to him and celebrated Malik's amazing goal.

The game, once again, was tied.

The minutes ticked slowly off the clock. Play was even. Neither team could gain an advantage or put another ball into the net. Reggie, Omar, and the Gators' defense held strong. Malik and his fellow forwards put some pressure on the Raiders goalie but never made a shot good enough to get past him.

With just a few minutes left in the game, Malik knew he and his teammates would have to act fast to avoid a tie.

"Increase the pressure!" he yelled as the ball drifted out of bounds. Omar went for the throw-in. "Let's give it everything we've got!"

Malik sprinted toward Reggie in the middle of the field. "Show them your moves," he told him. "Be more aggressive, okay?"

"Okay." Reggie was panting.

Malik placed his hand on his neck. "I want you to get the ball. Then when you do, keep control and work your way to the goal. Get past your defender and I'll get open for the pass."

"What if I can't get by him?" asked Reggie

"You will," insisted Malik.

"But if I lose the ball, it'll leave us vulnerable on defense," said Reggie. No one played behind him. If Reggie gave up the ball, the Raiders could make a run the other direction.

"You won't lose it." Malik turned and raced back into position. He turned toward Reggie. "I believe in you!"

As Malik got into position near the box, the throw-in came to Reggie just across the centerline. His defender gave him room. Reggie kept his head up and looked across the field. *You can do it, Reggie*, thought Malik. *Show us what you've got.*

Reggie drifted forward, keeping the ball close to his foot. Then, in a flash, he made his move. He dribbled toward the defender, faked his entire body to the left and went right. The defender froze. He could only watch as Reggie shot past him.

Another Raiders defender came over to meet Reggie. *One more*, thought Malik. *One more good move.* At this point he was looking for his own opening. He was making sure he was in position when Reggie was ready to deliver a pass.

Reggie was near the box. This time he beat his defender by faking a shot. He brought his right foot backward and sold the move. The defender went for the block. Reggie quickly moved around him and again went right.

Malik rushed toward the net and raised his arm. Reggie saw him and led him with a pass. It was right on target. Malik collected the ball, took one look at the goalie, and then put everything he had into the shot.

He heard the sound he loved—the sound of soccer cleat meeting soccer ball in one vicious blow. The ball sailed toward the net. The goalie stretched out for the ball but couldn't reach it. Malik's shot went past him and hard into the webbing of the back of the net.

His teammates mobbed him. In their excitement, they all piled on top of Malik and took him to the ground. Malik couldn't stop smiling.

As the pack cleared off him, Malik stood up and found Reggie. "Excellent moves out there," he said. "That was exactly what I wanted you to do."

"It was pretty awesome, wasn't it?" Reggie laughed.

Malik laughed too. "It sure was."

He turned to the rest of the team. "Okay, no letting up!" he shouted. "We need to play tough defense. This game is almost over, but we have to play hard until the final whistle!"

Malik's teammates did just what he asked. Their defense was a wall, and the Raiders never had another serious scoring opportunity the rest of the game. The referee blew his whistle and the game was over. They had beaten the

Raiders 3–2. They had gotten their first win under Coach Howard.

After the postgame handshakes, Malik found Coach Howard. "Hey, Coach," he said. "You're all right, you know that?"

Coach Howard laughed. "Well I'm glad you think so."

Malik smiled. "And I really am sorry for how I acted when you first came here. I was wrong not to give you a chance."

"It's forgotten," said Coach. "The future's all I care about."

"I hear that."

Malik then jogged over to Omar and Reggie. "Awesome win, guys! You made me proud."

"Hey, Malik," said a voice behind him. Malik turned. It was the two scouts from East Coast University.

"Great play out there," said one of them.

"You showed awesome leadership," said the other. "That was obvious from the sidelines."

"Thanks," said Malik.

"Before you leave the field," said one of the scouts, "come talk to us. We'll be waiting on the bleachers." The scout looked at Reggie. "We'd love a word with you as well."

Reggie got a huge grin on his face. Omar gave him a playful shove. "Our newest superstar!" Omar teased.

As the scouts walked away, Malik elbowed Reggie. "East Coast U. That's big time. Maybe we'll be teammates again one day."

"We'll see," said Reggie.

Malik put his arms around Omar and Reggie.

"What do you say we keep this winning streak going?" he said. "Keep it going all the way to the state title?"

"Sounds good to me," said Omar.

"I'm down." Reggie smiled.

The three guys walked toward their teammates. It was time to celebrate.

ABOUT THE AUTHOR

Chris Kreie is an elementary school teacher in Eden Prairie, Minnesota. He's an avid sports fan and outdoorsman who especially enjoys hiking and camping near Lake Superior along Minnesota's north shore. He lives in Minneapolis with his wife and two children.